—

The Same Beat

Dakota Britton-Barrows

An imprint of Enslow Publishing

WEST **44** BOOKS™

**Please visit our website, www.west44books.com.
For a free color catalog of all our high-quality books,
call toll free 1-800-398-2504.**

Cataloging-in-Publication Data

Names: Britton-Barrows, Dakota.
Title: The same beat / Dakota Britton-Barrows.
Description: New York : West 44, 2022. | Series: West 44 YA verse
Identifiers: ISBN 9781978595606 (pbk.) | ISBN 9781978595682
(library bound) | ISBN 9781978595620 (ebook)
Subjects: LCSH: Children's poetry, American. | Children's poetry,
English. | English poetry.
Classification: LCC PS586.3 B758 2022 | DDC 811'.60809282--dc23

First Edition

Published in 2022 by
Enslow Publishing LLC
29 East 21st Street
New York, NY 10011

Editor: Caitie McAneney
Designer: Katelyn E. Reynolds

Photo Credits: Cvr E.R. Images/Shutterstock.com; cvr, pp. 1–196
(torn newspaper) STILLFX/Shutterstock.com; p. 136 (note) ESB
Professional/Shutterstock.com; p. 180 (postcards) MM_photos/
Shutterstock.com.

Printed in the United States of America

CPSIA compliance information: Batch #CW22W44: For further information contact
Enslow Publishing LLC, New York, New York at 1-800-398-2504.

This book is dedicated to my family for always accepting me for who I am, and to my wife, for giving me the courage to write these words.

For young queer people finding their way in this world, this book is also for you.

A Typical Day

I hear my parents
shuffle around
the house.
Get ready for work.

I hear the soft hum
of an engine.
Tires briefly stopping.
The creak of the
the mailbox door opening.
The car continuing on.

The newspapers have arrived,
and I race to grab them.

Reading

My parents joke that
I am an older person
trapped
in a younger body.

Reading a newspaper
with breakfast.
Pausing for a sip of coffee
between paragraphs.

Trying to take in as much
of the real world
as I can.

My Ride

My best friend Maria
picks me up in her
beat-up station wagon.
It's a hand-me-down
from her grandmother.
It's still perfect to
get us to where
we need to go.

Our Spot

We gather with our classmates in front of the
school doors,
waiting for first period to start.
I am still catching up
on the day's headlines
on my phone.

Maria pulls a small mirror
out of her purse,
applying the makeup
that her mother won't allow.

I Pretend

that the buzzing chatter
around me is a newsroom.

That everyone is grabbing their
coffees, rushing to their desks.

Pounding on their keyboards
until they are released from the room
like lightning bugs from a mason jar.

Ready to explore the world
with fresh eyes.

Circle

Our circle
is filled with people
who are mostly there
to talk to Maria.

I jump into a
conversation
every so often.
But mostly I keep
reading,
even if they
call me a nerd.

Maria Is Semi-Popular

She acts like she's not.
But she has boys
ask her out weekly.
And the popular girls
ask her to hang out on
the weekend.

They always say,
*You can bring Teegan
if you want.*

Maria and Teegan

We met in the fifth grade,
when we had all the
same classes
and Maria still had
the gap between her front teeth.

When she got picked on
so bad that I was the
only one who
stood up for her.

Now she
stands up for me.

On the Weekends

We go to the park
or the lake.

We lie in the sun
on a blanket we
keep in the car.
Pack snacks
and watch people
go about their day.

We read side by side.
Fall asleep sometimes,
with the smell of grass
inching toward our faces.

We show each other
funny videos we
find online and laugh
until our cheeks burn.

It's so simple
and perfect.

It's us.

Black and White

Even though the print
is always in
black and white,

facts and truth,

stories are not as
simple as that.

There's always a gray area.
Is this person a bad person?
Or did they just do a bad thing?

Those are the stories I crave.

A dig into the background,
a dive into the deep end,
a trail of information
with no end in sight.

Maria Now

Straight teeth;
chestnut brown hair,
long and wavy;
hazel eyes;
olive skin;
dark, edgy clothes
that hang from
her thin body.

Her personality
could keep you
warm in the winter.
She has a laugh
that could make
you feel like it's summer
all year long.

How I See Myself

I would trade
my plain brown hair
for a blonde
that would bring out
my green eyes.

I would add an inch or two
to my height
to stand taller.

I would research "style"
so that I could say that I had one.

Cut these jeans to fit better,
feel good in a tight shirt.

I would take this frown
and replace it with a smile

so bright
that I could light up
this whole town.

After School

I go to
the newspaper
meeting.

Maria goes to
the photo club
meeting.

We meet at the
station wagon after.

Maria wants to know
what I'm writing. I am
always writing something—

poems, short stories, news stories.

So I give her my latest beat—
my special news assignment—
to look at.

She shows me
her new photos.

We crank the radio
all the way home.

Sometimes

we have dinner as a family,
and sometimes my parents
work late and I order takeout.

I retreat to my room.
Return to the open books
on my walnut-stained desk.
Dive into researching
my next article:

```
The Effects of Cliques on Teenagers
```

Everyone Has a Story

Their own history,
likes, dislikes,
complex emotions.

It interests me to watch
how these stories cross into
others.

How we are one person
but have a part in
so many other
lives.

How it matters
what we do with our chapter.

This Summer

When this summer
came up
in conversation
with Maria,
I never expected
it to be different
from all the others.

I figured we'd spend it
like we always do—
together.

But She's Leaving Me

Maria tells me she's going
on a road trip this summer

to all the colleges
she might want to attend.

She seems so excited,
so set on success.

And I already feel like
she's leaving me behind.

When We Were Younger

Maria said we'd be together forever,
go to college together,

live next door to each other,
have babies at the same time.

Our lives would be on the same track,
like we were married to each other.

But here she is, telling me about her plans
and not inviting me.

And it hurts to know
that there will be an end.

She will go her way.
I will go mine.

There Will Be a Day

when she won't be there for me.
Or maybe it'll be me
who gives up on us.

Either way, I'm not ready
for the heartbreak
of letting her go.

I Tell My Parents

that I want to be productive this summer.
That I need to figure out my plans.
That I need to be okay without my best friend.

I am freaking out.

I
can't
just
stay
here
without
her.

I need my own plans,
my own path,
my own dreams.

I can't put myself second anymore.

My School

buzzes
with excitement
as summer approaches.
Everyone feels antsy.
It's windows-down,
music-up-loud
kind of
weather.

We are all waiting
to feel free.

Candlewood Lake

is the lake of my childhood.
So soft in the sunshine,
velvet ripples,
calming.

There's me, always observing,
never wading in,
not interested in breaking
the steady waves.

Everyone else runs on the docks.
Everyone else jumps in.

I wonder if I'll ever
be brave enough
to make a splash.

I Tell Maria

I feel
different,
restless,
reckless.

She asks me
if it has anything
to do with her
leaving.

Goodbyes

I stay silent because I don't know what to say.
I don't want to tell her how betrayed I feel.

She swallows me in a hug and tells me
she wishes I could come with her this summer.
How it's not going to be the same without me.

But she never says why
she needs to go so far
that I can't follow.

Why she suddenly chose
a different path
when I thought we
were on the same road.

Maria Is Excited

for her college tour.

She tells me all about the campuses of:

Syracuse
Elmira
Ithaca
Penn State
Ohio State
Kent State—

every state

that isn't here
in Connecticut

or within a
two-hour commute
of Brookfield.

I Am Afraid

that once she leaves,
she's not going to come back.

Not the same Maria
that I've known since
fifth grade.

Maria isn't the type
who only belongs in the city
or in the country.

She just belongs everywhere,
can get used to anything.

She becomes part of the scenery.
Part of the hustle and bustle.

Maria makes friends with
the squirrels or pigeons,
the ants on the sidewalks.

She's going to be fine
wherever she goes.
I just wish I could say
the same for me.

My Parents Have News

Teegan, your Mom and I have
exciting news
about this summer.
I talked to my friend
in New York City.
How does a journalism camp sound to you?

Stay in a private room there,
          in a dorm with other teens.
I know you like alone time,
          but this is an opportunity
to spread your wings
          and meet new people!

It's Weird

when you start
to remember
how lonely
going out
into the world
feels.

Maria Is Happy for Me

when I tell her
about the camp.

I can hear in her
voice that she's trying
not to be jealous
that I found a way
to replace her
so fast.

The hole is still there, though.
Just knowing I have to face
the real world
without my best friend.

Headlines

are my favorite
thing to write.

Words to catch your attention.
Reel you in.
Keep you until the end.

I have yet to create a
headline
bold enough
for myself.

So I Pack

I take my favorite things.

I pack the photos of
me and Maria,
my mom and dad.

I zip my suitcase.

...

An hour and a half until I create
a new headline
for my life.

Jitters

I've been to the city a handful of times
    before,
        but this time
            feels different.

    The butterflies in my stomach
    are
    dancing
    wildly
    to
    a
    song
        I can't hear.

My Eyes

shuffle past the buildings.

    So fast
        that I can't
            tell them apart.

    But I am here,
    and I am in it.

Millions of people are around me.
    I can feel our existence vibrate under me.

        We are here together
            and lonely at the same time.

I miss Maria,
    but I look out onto Fifth Avenue
        and see a promise I have to keep
        to myself.

Empty

I drag myself into the room
that will be my new home
for the next two months.
A single-bed dorm room
with a small writing desk.

White walls.

Empty until now.

Who was here before?

I wonder.

It's so

      quiet.

Just how I like it.

Mr. Martin

is teaching our
journalism class.

He wears suspenders
and glasses.
Sports a mustache,
just like my father.

They've been friends for years,
my father and Mr. Martin.

This is the first time
I've ever met him.

Welcome, Teegan.
I look forward to getting
to know you this summer.

There's This Boy in the Corner

talking quietly with another girl.
Making her laugh.
Creating curiosity in the room.

He's cute:
tall,
brown hair,
pretty eyes.

I hear him say
his name is Bill.

He blinks his blue eyes
like a camera
snapping.

Shannon

is very chatty.
The first one
to approach me
and introduce herself.

I sit next to her and
listen to how
she got here.
Her love of the news,
of the city.

She wants to start over
in a place where no one
knows her name.

She thinks this is it.

I believe her, too.

Shannon Has Moved On

Making a point to meet every
single student in our class.

I sit silently,
taking out my notebook
and my favorite pen.

I don't look up

until—

is **bold** and *italic*.
Her eyes <u>underlined</u>
with purple instead of black.
Her wild hair does not apologize.

She moves like a highlighter,
marking all the important
information you need to know:
where she's been,
where she's going.

When she smiles
at you,
you're going to forget
your own name.

As if you've been saying hers
your whole life.

Refocus

The class starts.

Mr. Martin explains
how this summer will go.
How we will meet every day
to learn how to write
like a journalist.

We'll be assigned a new beat each week.
We'll be partnered up.
Then we will be set free
to get a jump on the story.
Let our creativity run wild
in the streets
of New York City.

The Final Project

A whole newspaper
made up
of every article
we write
this summer
with our
beat partners.

Mr. Martin's Summer Assignment:

Write

your

hearts

out.

Chatter Fills the Room

Shannon turns to me. Says,
Think of all the amazing things
we're going to be able to do!

Bill leans over and adds,
It'll look great in
our portfolios!

Marcy looks over,
doesn't say a word.
But her face seems
to be smirking, as if
she's saying,
I know something
you don't know
yet.

The Basics

Mr. Martin introduces the basics
of journalistic writing.

Leads.
Facts.
Truth.

Leave your opinion out of it.

That's easy—

I've been doing that my whole life.

After Class

A small group of classmates
gather outside when we
are released.

Hey, Teegan! Come join us.

I think that must be Shannon.
The friendly one.
But I turn around to
see Marcy waving me over.

I take a deep breath
and walk over to them.

Some Girl Named Willow

suggests that we should
try to get into a bar.
She knows a place
in Greenwich Village
that has a spoken-word
open mic tonight.

She wants to go where the cool
kids go. But speaking poetry
was never cool in *my* school.

I like New York already.

The Village

is exactly how I
imagined
it would be.

There is an unspoken
scent in the air
that attracts misfits,
artists, poets.

We find ourselves here
before we
even know
where we
are going.

Bill Asks the Table

if anyone wants a drink.

He's tall and charming
enough to get away with
ordering one.

I say, *No, thanks.*

Marcy turns to
me and smirks. *You like to follow the
rules, don't you?*

I answer,
*I'd just rather not get arrested
my second night
in New York.*

Willow chimes in,
*Haven't you heard?
This is
the City!
Here,
you are free!*

The Performer

makes her way up to the mic.
Holds the stand like she is
depending on it for strength.
Closes her eyes
and begins.

Her Words

are like darts
flying at the wall.
Every sentence sticks.
The emotion of each
line can be seen on her face
by the way her lips reach up
to light her eyes.
Or the way they drop down
toward her chin.

Her face is a poem,
and the audience
is reading it all.

I Am Twinkly-Eyed

with a hint of tears
pushing up against
the barriers of my
eyelids—glowing,
like a light switch
turned on
in a rainy night.
Glowing softly
in the silence.

My Newfound Friends

exclaim in wonder,
chatting about what
a great show it was.

They are loud,
cutting off my train
of thought.

As always,
I keep my wonder
to myself.

I'm trying to figure out
how someone could
put words together like that
and then deliver them out loud.
So beautifully, it's like
watching flowers
bloom right in
front of you.

The Next Morning

I have subway cars
riding around
in my stomach.

We find out our beat partners today.

Then the real adventure

begins.

The Same Beat

Teegan and Marcy! You two are beat partners.

The class turns to look at me.
Like I won the lottery.
I know what they're thinking...

That I don't deserve to be partners
with someone who looks like
they know the world.

Could get you into the coolest parties.
A-list celebrity status.

You can almost hear champagne

p p i   g
  o p n

every time she's in the room.

The First Meeting with Marcy

Marcy speaks **boldly**.

Hey, Teegan! Are you excited for this summer?
We didn't get to talk much last night.

Where
are
you
from?

We're going to have fun with this!

I'm from Ohio.
Graduated this June.
Not going to college in the fall.
Decided to do this camp last minute,
so when I go backpacking through Europe,
I can write all about it. Report my days
like news stories.

Have you ever been to Europe?

I'm Not Sure

if she can tell she overwhelms me.

Before I can answer, the teacher tells us
to get to know our new partners.

To do that, our first assignment is to
interview them and write a profile.

Thanks to Marcy's intro,
I am already halfway done.

Overloaded

Marcy's personality
takes up so much space
in a room, you always know
she's there.

I'm not sure where
I fit in.
Why I am here

or what I have to
contribute.

How will I even
compare?

Where Should We Start?

You go first,
I insist,
as if she hasn't
already.

So she continues.
And even though she talks
so fast,
I catch every word,
every twitch of her cheek
when she talks about her future plans.
How she will never go back
to Ohio.
How she will travel
her whole life,
start a blog,
inspire millions of people.
Maybe become a tour guide
or a professor.

Her eyes get so wide when
she talks about each thing
she hopes to accomplish.

My Turn

Should I tell her the truth?
About how I am not sure
I am even a whole human?

Should I tell her I spent most of
my life living in shadows,
making sure my footprints
matched those in front of me?

How my best friend left me
and I feel so empty?
How I left my hometown
and I feel so detached?

Or maybe I should tell her
that I am a world traveler.
I am an archaeologist
digging up the pasts of the people
who have lived before me.

Looking for any place I can call home.

I Start with What I Know

> I just turned 17 and
> I'm graduating next June.
> I'm an only child
> from Connecticut.
> I like writing and photography
> and any art, really.
> I read the news every morning.
> I have never really been on my own.
> But, uh, maybe don't write that.
> That's lame.

She laughs. Says,

Okay, but tell me something real now.

> *Real?*

Yes. What makes you YOU?

> *I—I don't know.*

What's special about you?

> *I—I don't know. I'm just me.*

It's okay, we'll get you there.

Yet

Mr. Martin begins:

Okay, class.
I hope you enjoyed your first assignment!
You will eventually turn them in.
But first you have to exchange
the piece you've written
about your beat partner
with them.

After you're done reading,
you will pass them in to me.

At the end of this program,
you will write another one
to compare how much you've learned
about one another.

There will be a lesson in this,
but we're not there yet.

Sharing

I have a lump in my throat.
How did I not know
we would have to share?

I hope Marcy doesn't hate it.
Oh God, what did she write about me?
There was nothing to write about...

Marcy hands me her piece and winks.
Walks away with mine.

I close my eyes and swallow.
Here we go.

A Profile on Marcy

Marcy is bold for her age:
a recent high school graduate
looking for the excitement
of adventure.

Unsure of what she wants to do,
she plans on backpacking
through European countries
in search of her meaning
and purpose.

She is confident in her
direction though,
as if she
controls the wind,
ready for takeoff.

A Profile on Me

The city is on the brink of dusk
as Teegan cradles her coffee mug in her hands.

She is unsure about spilling
too much about herself,
aware of how very little she finds
exciting in her life.

The nervousness in her voice reveals her secret:
she is an unfinished draft, a work in progress, a
writer blinded by a blank page.

Teegan is a 17-year-old girl in search of herself.
This is not to say that she is lost in the crowds, but
that she is just realizing her ability to shine.

Teegan is about to embark on an important
adventure—
a summer that will teach her
that she holds the pen.

I Sit for a While with Marcy's Words

Mr. Martin asks if everything is okay.
I am in such a fog that I didn't know
everyone had left already.

I get up and hand him Marcy's profile on me.

You know, Teegan,
first impressions are important.
But so is finding more information.

    Okay.

Get to know each other.

But—
what did she *mean*
by her words?

An unfinished draft?
A work in progress?

I Step Out of the Class

Hey, Marcy says.

I just wanted to make sure
you didn't get the wrong idea...
About what I wrote.
I think you're great.
But you can also rewrite
your whole life
right now, this summer.

> I tell her:
> *But I don't know what that means, Marcy.*
> I feel cornered into change.

Her head tilts.
I swear I see Times Square
lit up in her eyes.

Let me show you.

I Want to Go Home

Back where I can be me
and no one is trying to
tell me who to be.

This is why I was
afraid of Maria
leaving.

Who am I without her?

I Fight the Urge

to call my parents
and ask them to
send me home.

I need to face Marcy
head on and understand
what she thinks
she sees in me
that I can't yet.

Sports Beat

Marcy tells me she's never been to
a baseball game.
That I will have to write most of
this beat.

But she has other questions.

*Alright, so is it too corny to ask
what team you bat for,
since we're at a baseball game?*

> *What do you mean?*
> *They bat for their own team.*

*No, not the players. You.
For example, I bat for both teams.
As in...
I'm bisexual.*

> Oh. Oh. OH. *That's* what she means.

Wow

She really just
came out
and said it.

To an almost
complete
stranger.

It's not like
I don't know
queer people.

It's just that I haven't
met anyone so
bold and forward
about it.

Maybe because people
where I'm from
can be so mean about
things like—

Teegan?

*Oh, I—well, I've only ever batted for one
team.
The straight one?
So ... I guess ...*

I am tripping
      over
my own
            tongue.

How can I explain
my lack of a dating life
to this worldly person?

Marcy laughs.
*Don't feel the need to answer.
It's okay.*

> *Do you have a
> boyfriend, girlfriend,
> uh ... friend?*

Marcy's Laugh Is a Billboard

An advertisement.

You don't know what she's selling,
but you want to buy it.

You're so cute. Well, I am single.
Wild and free as a bird!
The way I like it.

A baseball
        cracks
against a bat.

OH WOW! Is that a...
touchdown?

        My turn to laugh.

        That would be a home run, dear.

Marcy smirks at me,
and suddenly my stomach is
a popcorn machine.

Marcy Is at My Door

first thing in the morning.
All I hear is the knocking,
but I know it's her
by the way she does it—

brightly announcing herself
and asking permission
at the same time.

I open my eyes into a sliver.
Roll out of bed and open the door.

Look at her shining with
the golden reflection of the sun,
barely breaking the
line of skyscrapers
beyond my window.

Hey. She's smiling.
I brought you coffee.
Come with me.

The Roof

And that is how I find out
our dorm building
has roof access.

And that is how I find out
that Marcy's favorite
time of day is sunrise.

And that is how I find out
that teenage girls can fly,

as long as they can see the sky.

Sleepy

I keep nodding off in class.
Can't keep my head up
on my fist.
Dreaming of my bed.
Until I hear the softness of my name,
rocking me awake.

While I Was Dozing

Marcy fills in
the gaps.

Mr. Martin gave us press passes
for an exhibit opening
at the MoMA tonight!

Have you ever been there?

We should change and
then go!

I told Bill and
Shannon we'd meet
them there.

We Meet in the Lobby

I'm wearing a blue pantsuit
that I bought last year
because it looks like something
female news anchors wear.

In case any such occasion
occurred,
I would be prepared.

This is one such occasion.

But Marcy walks down
the stairs
wearing a stunning emerald dress
with a silver necklace.
A fancy barrette in her
perfectly curled hair.

She looks more beautiful
than any artwork
I have ever seen.

The Museum of Modern Art

is humming,
and we are
in the middle
of it all.

I am
excited,
nervous,
happy.

I don't remember
the last time
I felt
all three
at once.

Starry Night

I can feel a pulse
coming from
the walls.

Marcy is starry-eyed.
She keeps her pen ready
and her notebook open.

Hey, can we go see Van Gogh? I ask.
Before the opening ceremony starts?

Oh right. Sure!
Let's just make it back in time
to get a good spot.

We climb the stairs
and walk toward my favorite
painting in the world—

Starry Night.

Magic

It is pure magic
that I am witnessing it
with my own eyes.

It's so beautiful.

You like?

I love.

My Confession

Marcy watches my wonder.
I decide to explain.

Whenever I'm going through a tough time,
I go on my porch, shut off all the lights,
and look out at the stars.
They calm me.
They make me believe
that I am both small and big.
That I can conquer anything.
That I can create anything.
That I could burn so bright,
someone else could SEE me.
I know it sounds lame,
but I really, really do love staring
into space and pretending the
stars are looking back.

Marcy's eyes turn
from starry excitement
to a misty twinkle.

For once,
her voice is a whisper.

That's not lame at all.

Marcy Drops Me Off

at my room later.
Fidgets with her bag.
As if she doesn't know
what to say.
That's not her style.

You okay?

I just had a really great time with you tonight.
I loved that you were able to open up to me.
You're usually so … closed off.

I had a great time too.
But just so you know, I'm not closing myself
off to you.
I'm just more of an observer.

I see her slightly roll her eyes.

What?

I just think you deserve to let yourself …

Feeling cornered again,
I snap—

Marcy, why do you feel like you need to fix
me?

She is taken aback.

So Am I

My eyes start to well up.

I've been told so many times before
that I'm a nerd, that I'm too quiet.
I don't need your input too.

Okay, I'm sorry!
I've just been in your shoes before.
And it's always felt like a cage.

But I'm not you, Marcy.
And I can take care of myself.

Okay, Teegan.
You're right. You're not me.
I know who I am, and
I'm not afraid
to let people know it.

She stares at me for an extra moment.

Sorry I tried to help.

And just like that, she's gone.
Down the hallway, into the darkness.

In the distance, I hear a door slam.

I Don't Know Why...

I can't let anyone in.

I don't know why I get so mad
when someone tries to crack
the combination.
To get me to tell truths about myself
I've kept hidden away for years.

I keep reminding myself that Marcy will be gone
in a month.

That if I let her in now,

I'll have another hole to fill.

Texts from Maria

Hey bestie! I miss you so much!
I'm having a blast on my road trip,
but wish you were here.

Here is a collection of pics
from all the places I've gone.
Feel free to Photoshop yourself in.
I left room for you ;)
Let me know how your
journalism camp is going!
I can't wait to hear all about it!

Love you!
:*

It Hurts

to miss Maria.

My chest hurts
when I think about her.

She would never
ask me to change.

To open up.
To be louder.
Bolder.

But I realize something.

She would want me to.
She would want me to grow.

I Plan My Apology

but I can't get it right.
Maybe I should text Marcy—
that way I can edit as I go.
She won't have to sit through
my blabbering.

Okay, short and sweet.
But mostly sweet maybe.
Will she even forgive me?
Can we still be beat partners?
I should have never snapped at her.
I ruined everything.
Oh, God, I'm going to have
to tell my parents I want to
come home early.

And then how will I fill the rest of
my summer?

I can't do that.

I Open My Door

And there's a bag sitting out
in the hallway with my name.

When I open it,
my planned-out apology
fades away.

I open the tissue paper
to reveal a journal
covered in constellations,
with a note inside saying:

Follow your own stars.
No one can tell you
that you're lost.

Love,
Marcy

For the First Time

I am racing to class,
my heart beating
hard against my ribs.
I am bursting with emotion.
I don't know whether to laugh or cry
or hug a stranger
or still apologize.

All I know is that
I have to see Marcy
and she has to see me,
and I have to let her know
that everything is okay.

I Find Her

She's sitting in the classroom already.
I check my watch to make sure we have time.
I crack the door wider
and ask her to come outside.

Hey.

> *Hey.*
> *Listen, I am SO sorry*
> *I blew up at you.*
> *I never do that with anyone—*

No, it was my fault, I pushed you—

> *You were just trying to be a good—*

I should have given you space—

> *I got your present—*

I hope you liked it—

> *It was everything.*
> *Thank you.*

I Invite Marcy

over to my room
after dinner.
To seal our truce.
Give her a glimpse inside
my world:

stacks of books,
an exploding suitcase of clothes,
loose papers on my desk
that spill onto the floor.

Look at all these stories!
she exclaims,
as she discovers
my stash of
just-for-fun
writing.

I let her dig
a little deeper.

We Are Mapping Out

our remaining subjects,
what we have left to cover,
how much of the city we have yet to touch.

> *So I think we should do our history beat on*
> *like, Stonewall or something.*
> *Ellis Island? The Strand?*
> *I don't know, you pick.*
> *Marcy—are you sleeping?*

Just a little.
Give me a minute, okay?
I'll move to my room in a few.

> *It's so early! I figured you were a night owl.*

I like sunrises, remember?

> *You can sleep here if you want.*

Will you stay with me?

Sleeping Close

I don't know where she thought
I was going. But before I can answer,
she's asleep again.

I don't move.
I don't breathe.
I don't ... know.

I am lying a pencil tip away from her hand.
I can feel the heat coming from her body.
I can barely hear her soft snores over
the heavy beating of my own heart.

The sirens from the street can't even compete.

I stare at the ceiling,
wondering where this feeling
came from and if it's going to go
away.

If it does,

will I chase it?

Or will I let it go?

I Tell Myself:

I just miss Maria.
I'm just so happy to have a new friend.
It's just been a long day.
Maybe I miss physical touch.
Maybe I am tired.
Maybe my body was cold alone.
Maybe I am happy to have warmth.
Maybe I like …
Maybe she likes …
Maybe the summer is sinking in too quick.
Maybe I'm the cover-up to my own story.

Marcy Starts to Stir

I pretend to sleep.
She's trying to be quiet.
The sun is starting to rise.

Her favorite time of day.

I pretend to wake up,
even though I haven't slept
all night.

She apologizes for crashing,
for waking me so early.

I say it's no big deal.

It's a beautiful day.

No Sleep

For someone who didn't sleep,
I am amped.
My energy could power
our entire subway ride.

Marcy is quiet.
Distant.
Hollow in the eyes.

So not like her.

> *Hey, are you okay?*

*Sorry, yes, I am. I'm just feeling bad about
last night.*

> *Why do you feel bad?*

*I shouldn't have crashed at your place.
I'm sorry if I made you uncomfortable.*

> *Marcy, you didn't make me
> feel uncomfortable.
> At all. I promise.*

But I'm...

> *I know you like girls.
> It's okay. I'm okay. You're okay.*

Me. Comforting. Her.

What a concept.

Weeks of Adventure

If our weeks added up to anything,
it would be a flip book
of smiles,
exploration,
open mic nights
reeling us in.

Hurried hands writing
in slim notebooks,
using all punctuation marks,

beat by beat
by beat.

Interviews with shop owners.
Research at the library,
art galleries, museums,
Central Park, food carts,
the boroughs and the buildings.

My world bursting with stories.

Marcy's brilliant mind
and my steady hand—

a masterpiece in the making.

The Days

don't seem long enough.

In the heat of summer,
time is melting away.

Each day mixes with
the next until, before you
know it, I am a puddle
draining back into
Candlewood Lake.

Check In

Mr. Martin wants to know
how it's been going
on our beats.
How we've been working
with our partners.
How every story we write
will come together
in its own little newspaper.

Make sure to cover all the subjects.

Our final project.

We are more than halfway through
our eight-week program.

The summer dwindling.
Our friendship blooming.

So I'd say it's going well,
but too fast.

Voice

A group of my classmates
are standing outside,
debating what to do
and where to go.

A bar? A restaurant? Times Square?
I stay to the side
because no one is asking
my opinion.

But then I remember
that I don't have to
go where everyone else
is going.

So I raise my voice
and tell them I'm going
to the Strand,
if anyone else wants to go.

And then I turn
to walk in that
direction.

18 Miles of Books

Marcy and Willow
are at my heels.

I feel like I'm leading
a parade down
Broadway.

Every step
bringing us
closer to where
I want to be.

The Stacks

Every which way
you look,
there are books.

I love being lost
in the titles.
In the scent of old
books, used books,
new books.

I feel like Belle
in *Beauty and
the Beast*.
Up on the ladder,
reaching for a
new adventure.

It makes me want to
write a book bursting
with stories
of heartbeat cities
and girls with wild hair.

Where Would You Rather Be?

That night
we are on the roof,
looking at stars.

They might be airplanes or towers,
but it doesn't matter—
they're all stars to me.

Marcy asks me,
in a perfect world,
where I'd rather be
than here.

She Wants to Be

in Venice,
eating cannoli,
watching streets flood
with the hopes and dreams
of those who roam them.

She wants
the romance of time
and the smell of espresso.
To be overcome by a place
with such history.

I Tell Her

I want to be somewhere
warm, that feels
magical and cozy.
Somewhere that's brand new,
but feels comforting.

Maybe New Orleans!
she cries.

We laugh at how excited
she sounds.

But Marcy doesn't know
that here,
with her,
is what I meant.

The Next Day

Maria calls.

Oh no—
I never replied to her texts.

> *Hello?*

Hey babe!
Guess where I am this morning?

> *I honestly have no idea ... Where?*

New York City.
Play hooky—
come hang out with me.

Hooky

I send Marcy a quick text saying
I can't come to class today.
That I'll catch up with her later.

I don't say why.

There is some part of me
that doesn't want them
to meet.

That doesn't want
my two worlds
to collide.

I try to swallow the
anxious feeling
in my stomach

and go meet Maria
at the diner on Seventh.

Maria and Her Mom

When I get to the diner,
Maria and her mom
are waiting.

I hug them both so tight.
Try to remember what home
feels like,
smells like.

The questions start.

I can't help but smile
as I tell them all about
my adventures in the city.

Maria's mom says,
Oh honey, you look like you're glowing.
New York is really doing wonders for you.

Can Maria tell
that I am different?

I feel different.

Sleepover

Maria is staying the night in the city.
Her mom is tired, and they need a break.

So I tell Maria she can stay in my dorm and
we can go explore the Village.
I'll have her back first thing in the morning.

I have a missed call from Marcy
and I am snapped back to reality.

She's going to want to meet Maria.

Committed

I tell Maria a shortened version
of Marcy and she laughs.

*So you're telling me, you've only made
one friend in this city of 8 million people?*

I bashfully say, *Yes, but she's a good one.*

To which Maria replies,
You always were so committed.

I Feel Judged

I *could* have more friends
if I wanted to.
I am not difficult
to be around.
I fit in where
I need to.

But I read the news.
And the more people
you know, the messier
life gets.

And I like clean.
I like predicting
what will happen
to me.

The Lede

is everything,
the experts say.

The first line of any story needs
to keep the reader reaching
for more.

A precise calculation of words.

I have to start defining myself.
I have to stop letting others
outline me and give away the end.

Even Maria.

Maria and Marcy Meet

in my dorm room.
Act polite and nice,
then wonder
where we'll go to dinner.

Okay, breathe, I tell myself.
They are both my friends.
And they can exist in the same
space and time.
This doesn't have to be weird.

> *Marcy, how about you pick? You know
> more places than I do...*

This way!
says Marcy,
taking the lead.

And then it happens ...
the claiming of territory,
the marking of a friendship.

Marcy laces her arm in mine,
and we lead the way to the restaurant.

Maria lags behind.

I Am so Nervous

that I barely
touch my meal.

Maria and Marcy
talk like new friends.
They trade stories
of me.

Marcy starts outlining
her plans for world travel,
with exclamations
and excitement.

I sit silently,
moving to find comfort
in my seat
every minute.

Marcy Leaves

Well, I really should get to bed.
We have a big day tomorrow!
I'll let you both catch up.
So nice to meet you, Maria!
Teegan, I'll see you tomorrow.

And then she hugs me.
Like it's the most natural thing
in the world and like we've been
doing it all summer.

But we haven't.

And I am covered with
goosebumps
and sweaty at the
same time.

Marcy's Deal

Maria asks me what Marcy's deal is.

I tell her Marcy is just bold. She's bright.
She's like an open book that never ends.

I tell her Marcy is helping me
a lot in figuring out
who I am.

*And what, I don't help you
in knowing who you are?*

She says it as a joke, but I don't think it is.

> *Maria, it's not like that. I'm just saying
> she has a different perspective.*

*Is that why you haven't talked to
me all summer?
Because she's a better friend?*

> *No! Not at all. Stop. I'm not comparing
> you two. You're my best friend and Marcy
> is my …*

Maria's Eyes Widen

Marcy is your what, Teegan?

       She's just my friend!

Okay. Sure.

       What do you mean by that?

I'm just saying you've been acting
strange all night. I think you're trying
to replace me and you're too afraid to tell me.

       Oh, like you were here for me this summer?

Woah. Where did that come from?

       I just want to know why
       all of a sudden UConn
       wasn't good enough.
       Why I wasn't good enough.

What are you talking about?

       We were supposed to go
       to college together!

Who says that I'm not going there?

       You just want to leave.
       You're traveling the country looking for an out!

Maria Looks at Me Differently

As if her eyes are asking me
to take back what I said.

What I feel.

But I can't.

*Do you even know what
YOU want, Teegan?*

She gestures for me to answer.

Still—
nothing.

My head is hanging.
I'm staring at my feet,
wishing they could
run.

The Second Time Maria Leaves Me

Silence between us.
For the first time
since fifth grade.
Then:

Just because I know what I want,
it doesn't mean I'm leaving you.
You need to figure out your path.

I can't do that for you. Neither can Marcy.

> This is too much.
> I feel myself shut down.
> My voice feels dead when I speak:
>
> *I'm going to get you an*
> *Uber to your hotel.*
> *You're leaving tomorrow anyway.*
> *Have a good rest of your summer.*

Teegan—

> *Don't.*

Maria's stare could burn my whole body
to the ground. I want to cry just
looking at her. But I don't.

I hold my head up. Look away.

Hear only the hollow sound
of the door slamming.

I Pick Up My Phone

just to make sure Maria got
into the Uber.

I stare at the screen,
wanting to tell Maria
I am sorry.

But the words are not there.
My hands are not ready.

I need to let her words sink in.

Late-Night Texts

Marcy, are you sleeping?

No. I was just thinking about you.
What are you guys up to?

I kicked Maria out. I'm a mess.

WHAT! Do you want me to
come over?

I don't want you to see me like this.

Teegan, you are safe with me.

I'm just not sure what
you could do.

I'm coming over with chocolate.
Be there in five.

The Chocolate Helps

I tell Marcy
what happened.

I put my head in my hands,
lean on my desk,
and start to cry.

I feel overexposed,
like a piece of film
left out in the sun.

> *She's right though, you know?*
> *I've never known what I wanted.*
> *She's always right.*

So prove her wrong, Teegan.

Marcy Is Lying Next to Me

Her arms are wrapped around me.
I am trying to remember where I am.

I'm emotionally hungover
and my eyes are burning
from crying so much.

Oh God, Marcy must really
think I am so dramatic.
But it's nice that she stayed.
I'm surprised she's still sleeping.

I whisper, *Hey, Marcy. Hey.*
And gently shake her.
Her eyes flicker open,
close again, and then
come to life.

Hey, you.

She gives me a sleepy smile,
and I feel so at peace.

How about some breakfast?

Cuddling

I've never had sleepovers
with anyone but Maria.

Sometimes we slept in the same bed,
but even then,
we never cuddled.

But Marcy is from a different place.
Marcy is a year older.
Marcy knows how to comfort someone
and not kick them to the curb.
Marcy knows how to hold me.
Marcy knows who she is.

The Big Question

You've barely touched your pancakes ...

> *Marcy ...*

Yeah?

> *How do you know who you are?*

She laughs, wipes her lips with the corner
of the napkin sitting in her lap and says,

Some days I do and some days I don't.
But the times when I feel most like myself
are when I get to choose what I want to do,
and I feel so free doing it.
It's almost hard not to smile.
I could be alone in a café,
drinking coffee, and just feel so ...
grateful, you know?

I remember the way it felt
to spend hours in Strand Books
and get a glimpse into
my own answer.

The Way She Sips Coffee

I watch Marcy inhale
French toast and eggs and bacon.
She is so cute when she
goes in for a sip.

She always blows on it,
even when it's cold.
Always lifts her eyes
to meet mine,
so when the liquid
finally reaches her lips,
we are staring at each other.
The corners of her lips start
to curl up toward the sky.

What?

>*What do you mean, what?*

You're smirking. Do I have something on my face?

>*You just look so happy. It's cute.*

Well, I am.
Happy, I mean.

And I am grateful.

For this moment.
And for her.

When I Was Little

I loved
spinning rides
at the fair.

Going around and around
until everything turned
into streaks of color.

New York is a tilt-a-whirl.
I can't seem to stop,
to slow down.

This summer is blurring,
and all I want is
to see clearly.

Back to Basics

Mr. Martin says:

Alright, class,
you should have all the
information you need
to complete your final
project.

I hope what you've gained
from this class is the ability
to tell what is fact and
what is story.
What is truth
and what is filler.

I hope you've learned that perspective is everything.

The more information and detail,
the better.

I hope you know that your job
is to let people know what's going
on around them.

Be accurate.
Be true.
But tell it in a way
only you can.

I Can't Believe

this class is almost over.
I have to go home soon.
I have to face Maria
and my senior year.

I'm not ready to say goodbye
to New York yet …
or Marcy,
or the "me" who
exists here.

I feel like I have so much
more exploring to do.
So much more of myself
to learn about.

And Marcy.
Why do I feel so sad
to leave her?

We still have two weeks left
and a whole newspaper to write.

It just doesn't feel like enough.

New Things

Marcy is leaning against the door
to my room with her notebooks
pushed up against her chest.

I ask her what she's up to tonight.

Well, I heard that Bill is having a party.
Would you want to go …?

    Sure! That sounds fun.

Really?

    Yeah, why not?

You weren't the party type when you got here.

    I'm not usually.
    But New York has me in the mood
    to try new things.
    I can't stay in my dorm forever.

That's my girl!
I'll come by around nine tonight.

    You won't be asleep?

She laughs,
pushes my arm.
Very funny.

The Party

We slide into the party
like we've been here before.

Marcy takes my hand
and slices the crowd in half.
Hands me a drink—
we clink our cups together.

The beer is gross,
but Bill and Shannon
sing its praises.

I leave to go to the bathroom.
When I come back out,
I wait in line for a refill
and scan the room for Marcy.

I see her sweet-talking
a tall boy by the window.

I see her throw her head back
in laughter and put her hand
on his arm.

I feel my cheeks turn hot.
Feel an army of tears
marching toward my eyes.

What's going on with me?

Marcy Sees Me

staring at her.
She reads my face.

I see her excuse herself
and come over to me.
But I turn around

and the tears find their weight
and start their free fall.

How Many Drinks Have You Had?

Marcy asks me,
concerned.

She puts her hand on
my back and leads me away
from the crowd.

Bill and Shannon look confused.

Marcy brings her hands to my face,
trying to look me in the eyes.
Searching for an answer is hard
when your source refuses to spill.

Please, tell me what's wrong.

How can I explain to her that I
don't even know the answer?

Marcy Guides Me

back to my room.
Tucks me into bed.
Lies next to me,
brushing my hair back
as I curl my face
into the pillow.

The Truth

is what reporters
hold sacred.

But right now,
it's the hardest thing
to admit to
myself.

Marcy Is Gone by Morning

There is a water bottle, Advil, saltines, and a note:

Teegan, you might feel awful this morning. Here are some things that will help.

Get some rest.

XO,

Marcy

I Stay in Bed for Most of the Day

Not even feeling sick,
just sad and torn.

What am I going to say to Marcy?
How do I explain why I was upset?

I don't even know why I was.

I just remember her flirting,
and ...I ... got ... angry. Desperate.

God, I am so territorial.
I really need to make more friends.

So I won't feel like people
are leaving me all the time.

But I never felt this way with Maria ...
not like *that*.

Twelve Hours Later

I haven't moved.

I have so many messages
from Marcy and Maria
and my parents.

I don't have the energy.
I can't stop my brain from
traveling down rabbit holes

of home

and here

and Maria

and Marcy

and who I've always been

and who I might be.

The Knot in My Stomach

holds something big

that my mouth does not

want to say.

Middle of the Night

and I am wide awake
thinking how

I have never considered
that I may be queer.
I always just thought
I liked being alone a lot.
Escaping into other
people's stories.

I am trying to unravel
what that means.
Trying to trace when it was
that I fell in love with Marcy.

Trying to figure out
why I tried to block
those feelings
from becoming
reality.

Journalism is about
finding the truth.
And it's been hiding
under my nose
this whole time.

What Will Maria Think

when I tell her
this revelation?

Will she wonder if
I was ever in love
with her, too?

That Afternoon

I start a letter
to myself.

I write and write

until I can't even believe
I am still holding the pen.

But I am.

I Get Dressed

I stand up.
I look in the mirror.
I look at my phone.
I reply to Marcy.

I am okay.

THANK GOD YOU ARE ALIVE!

As I read her text,
I can feel the lines on my face
where the tears have streamed
for the past two days.

I wish I could deny
the skyscraper of truth
in my gut.
But it keeps building up,
keeps trying to inch its way
out of my mouth.

Keeps trying to reach for the sun.

Last Beat

Inspiration strikes.

Suddenly, I am typing so fast.

My fingers so determined.

This is the best beat I've ever written.

That Night

I slide an envelope under Marcy's door.

I let her know where I'll be.

I feel free.

I feel free.

I Look for the Sunrise

It's cloudy, of course.
I lay out the blanket and
set up breakfast:

croissants
        baguettes
cannoli
        coffee mugs
juice

Anything that could give the
impression that we could be
in Europe.
Or anywhere but here.
Somewhere Marcy would
rather be,
but with me.

I hear footsteps coming up the stairs.

My heart is going to burst
like fireworks on the
Fourth of July.

Welcome to Café du Teegan!

I smile but Marcy looks serious.

I see you got my envelope.

I look down at my feet.

The skyscraper in my gut
feels like it's
crashing down.

Gone

Marcy comes close to me.
The sun starts to break through.
There are small patches of warmth
on my skin.
I am shaking from the inside out.

She leans in,
kisses me,
and there is a soft
silence between us
as our lips move
in waves.

I feel like an astronaut,
quietly floating off
into space and
landing among
the stars.

I never want to come
back down.

When I open my eyes,

all I see is her hair
dancing away.

She's gone before I can even say
a word.
As quickly as she came,
Marcy pulls away

without ever looking at me.

I Don't Go to Class

I don't want to see Marcy
until I know what to say.

My heart is in ruins,
and I am barely breathing
under the mess I've made.

I Text Marcy

Can we talk?

I am trying to understand
what happened
and I hope you can forgive me.

Please, text me back as soon
as you're comfortable.

She Finds Me in My Room

Hi.

> Hey, Marcy.

I'm so sorry for how I acted.
That profile ... was the nicest,
sweetest thing anyone has ever
done for me

... and that breakfast.

I'm sorry I didn't stay.
I'm sorry I kissed you.

> I'm not. Sorry that you kissed me, that is.

Teegan ...

> You don't like me, do you?

I do.
But I'm scared.

We Should Talk About This

We should talk through how we're feeling.
But instead I dare to be bold,
and I put my hands on her face.

She looks so different this close.
Like coming home after a tough day.

When I kiss her,
everything around me dissolves.

We are freestanding
and melting.

Wow.

She smiles.

    I smile.

It's time for the whole truth.

    I think I'm in love with you, Marcy.
    And it's terrifying.

    For the first time, though,
    I finally know what I want
    and who I am becoming.

    I uncovered my truth, and
    I have you to thank for that.

Marcy's Truth

She tells me,

*I just came out to myself within
the last year.*

So this is new to me, too.

*I'm not sure how this is supposed to go,
or where we go from here.*

We're both leaving so soon...

> I say,
> *We go to class, and we finish
> our assignment and figure
> out the rest later.
> For now, you and I
> are still on the same beat.*

I take her hand.

> *So, you're stuck with me.*

I Am Not

so calm and cool
when I close the door
and she leaves for the night.

I slump down in my chair
and think how
the last 24 hours have
happened so fast.
I have barely
caught my breath.

Marcy is amazing,
and I love her,
but I know
I could never
keep her with me.

She wants to be elsewhere.
She's always dreaming of more.

As she should be.

I Pick Up My Phone

and call Maria.

Hello? Teegan?

I sniffle back to real time.
My voice is cracking.

> *Maria. Hi. I'm so sorry.*
> *I just really need my*
> *best friend right now.*
> *Can you talk?*

I Tell Maria Everything

She replies without
missing a beat:

*Oh, babe, that makes more
sense than you realize.
I love you. Never forget that.
I'm here for you and
we are going to get that heart
of yours healed before school
starts again. You're going to
be okay. It may hurt now ...
but it's for the best ...*

Regret

I should have never told Marcy.

I am going to break both of our hearts

after I just brought them together.

I am a wrecker of my own church.

Build it up just to destroy it, just to

say I had prayed.

This is not who I want to be.

Marcy Is Different

So strange to me
in so many ways.
Like exploring a new country,
like learning a new language.
I could slowly create sentences
in her language.

Becoming familiar with her
led me to the deeper parts of her,
to the deepest parts of me.

Before being honest with myself,
I was lost in a shadow.

With Marcy, I am the light
beaming in the dark.

Last Week of Class

Marcy and I have to
finish our project.

Marcy and I have to
figure out how we'll leave off.

Marcy and I have to
figure out which punctuation
makes the most sense
for our story.

Smirking

I know we're okay
when I catch Marcy
smirk at me in class.

Like I'm the mug of coffee
in her hands.

Like she's trying to test the temperature
before swallowing me down.

Feelings

It is hard to know how I'm feeling.

About leaving.
         About Marcy.
About leaving Marcy.

About home.
About everything,
really.

I get so happy when I'm with her.
I get sad thinking about going home.

I don't know who I am there anymore.

Can I pack my new self to take with me?
Will I still be the same back in Connecticut?

Buried

I know there is only
one way to find the answer.

But the lede is buried—that is,
the truth of the story
is under wraps.

And I am looking
for the happy ending.

Marcy and I

spend almost all
of our time together.

Reaching for
each other's hands.
She grabs my waist
and pulls me
in close, just to
kiss me in the middle
of the crowded street.

Trying to create memories
in every corner
of this city.

Making sure
we will always
be this alive.

It is the bottom
of the ninth,
and we want
to go out swinging.

We Pull an All-Nighter

Editing and writing
our beats,
creating a newspaper
filled with our summer
adventures and
explorations.

And we are so tired
when the sun comes up
that we start laughing
at the spilled coffee on my floor
and the way my sweatpants
soak it right up.

I get up to change them,
turn away from Marcy to face
the corner of my room,
and turn back around to find
her staring.

I'm sorry, I didn't mean to stare …
Do you know how beautiful you are?

I immediately blush,
shake my head no.

You're more beautiful than the sunrise.
I'd rather wake up to you any day.

I believe her.

At the Printer

We are at the printer by 8:00 a.m.,
watching copies pour out of
the machine.

Warm paper,

sharp black ink.

Something concrete;

evidence

that this really happened.

Hot Off the Press

We read it like our story is today's news.
Like we have no idea what happened.
Like this summer was a dream
we're trying to remember.

Extra

We pass our paper out to the class,
watch them read the headlines—

extra, extra, read all about it!

I wonder if they can tell
we love each other,
just by looking at the way
the articles touch.

The way the edges
soften around our names.

The way every article
bleeds passion and hope.

In Conclusion

Mr. Martin says:

*What I hope you learned this summer
is that you can't trust first impressions.
Not for news articles. Not for people.
As promised,
I am going to have you write
a second profile on your beat partner.
When you're done,
please come up and hand them to me.*

*I will match it with your first one,
and give each of you both of the profiles
your partner wrote about you.*

*Compare them.
See how much it changed
once they got to know you,
got more details,
investigated your stories.*

Remember this:

*It's not about how much you think you know.
It's about what you know,
and the quest of knowing more.*

A Profile on Marcy, Pt. II

*Marcy beams with a glow of hope
as she talks about her future.
Reminiscing about being a child
with a dream to take flight
to Europe.*

*She has just stepped into
adulthood, freshly 18.
Ready to spread her wings.*

*New York City is just the first stop
for this jetsetter.*

*A tiny dot compared
to the rest of the world,*

*but what an impact she will make
on every place she will grace
with her footsteps*

*and every person who gets to
love her along the way.*

We Get an "A"

We go to our rooms to pack.
We are leaving tomorrow.
Straight to the airport for Marcy.
One-way ticket to Spain.

Straight to Connecticut for me.
One-way ticket to my past.

In Silence

We lie in bed,
Marcy's head on my chest.
She finally breaks the silence.

Teegan, what are we going to do?
I don't want to leave you tomorrow.

I think really hard before I answer.
Measure my words.
I don't want to mess this up.

> *We do what we have to do.*
> *You're going to go to Europe.*
> *I have to go home and finish*
> *my senior year.*

> *I have to figure out what the future*
> *looks like from there.*

> *We love each other.*
> *But we're not heading in the same*
> *direction right now.*
> *And that hurts.*

> *We're not on the same beat anymore.*

> *But—*

> *I can't wait to read your next*
> *story, Marcy.*

The Last Stop

I walk Marcy to the subway.
Help her carry her bags.
We don't say anything
until she turns to me.
She looks so sad,
so I joke about
how she'll forget about me
as soon as she boards
the plane.

Even that comes out sad though.

So I just get right to the truth:

> *Marcy … thank you.*
> *For everything.*
> *You never gave up on me*
> *and you offered me the most*
> *beautiful gift anyone can give*
> *another person.*
> *You showed me what love*
> *really feels like.*
> *I'm never going to for—*

No, don't say that.
That sounds too final,
like we're never going to
see each other again.
And I can't accept that.
I will think about you
all the time.

And I promise to tell you
everything.
I love you.

      I love you, too.

She kisses me,
turns away,
and I watch her
make her way
down the stairs
and disappear
into the station.

Candlewood Lake, Again

There she is:
the lake.

The memories
all seem distant now.

I see my classmates
all gathering
near the shore,
sunbathing,
soaking up every
last drop of summer.

I'm not who I used to be,
and I'm happy for it.

I stand on the dock and
close my eyes.

I feel
where Marcy
used to be.

I start to run,
make it to the edge,
and jump.

Finally
making
a splash.

Maria and I Share Stories

about our summers
away from each other.

I'm glad this is the one thing
that did not change.
The end of our friendship
would have been the worst.
We've only got more
room to grow.

Maria is thinking that
she'll apply everywhere,
see who gives her the
best deal.
Then she'll choose.

Said she liked all the places she went,
could see herself happy no matter
where she got in.

I try to imagine where I see myself.

I Dream About Riding Around

cobblestone streets on a moped
with Marcy.

We'd ride to the ocean,
and admire it,

the way
it continues to survive,

the way it
refuses to stop changing.

Maria asks me if I'm okay.
Asks if I know where I'm going to apply.

I say a city.
Maybe New York,
maybe Boston, or LA,
or even Chicago.

Somewhere with a heartbeat, you know?

February

Within three days,
they all come in.
Different envelopes
from different colleges.

I save them all to open
at once, let my fingertips
run over the emblem of the
school.

Feel the softness and
thickness of each one.

Try to identify the ones
with promise,
put aside the ones that look
like disappointment.

Postcards

I turn to look
at my bedroom wall,
a gallery
of postcards
from Marcy.

In the middle,
a collection of
Van Gogh postcards.

Each one with a message on
the back:

Sunflowers
Sunflowers remind me of you.
You're more beautiful
than you know.

The Bedroom
This one reminds me of your
dorm room
and all the nights I got to lay
beside you.

Café Terrace at Night
This one is self-explanatory, no?
;)

I Look at Myself

in the hanging mirror
in my room.
I have changed so much
just by opening myself up
to my truth.

More confident
in my posture.
I've learned to
stop looking down.

I wear T-shirts with
vests and khakis.
And it feels like they
fit just perfectly.

I Am a New Draft

with an open ending.

The ink setting in,
the printer idle,
the whole world waiting
for the morning paper

where I am the headline.

A Profile on Me, Part II.

Teegan holds a pen to her face,
looking down at the blank sheet
in front of her.

Teegan spent the summer
finding herself in artwork,
in street theater,
in poems echoing
down dark alleys,
in letting someone
compliment her.

I watch her from a few feet away.
She has inspiration in her eyes.

You can see that something has clicked.

She is ready.

She holds the pen down
and watches the ink spill,
jotting down everything
she has to say.

I Smile

when I think about Marcy
wandering faraway streets,
eating in cafes.

When I think about
how she drinks her coffee,
what art she's seeing,
all of the history
she's learning.

I smile

as I open my college letters.
One by one.
I leave the one I want most for last.

I peel back the paper,
feel it warm in my hand,
my palms so clammy that
the ink is starting to sweat with me.

I unfold the letter
and read:

It is with great pleasure...

I smile.

In This Moment

I know where I'm going.

And I just feel
so grateful,

you know?

Maria Leaves First

I wish we could
rewind the last year.

Maria and I
bursting
at the seams
of our town.

We would go on long drives
and explore new towns,
check out the art scenes,
find open mic nights.
Fill our hearts with dreams
that we didn't know we
could ever want
before now.

I Know Now

it would be wrong
if we both stayed.
If we followed our pact
to go to UConn together.

Senior year,

we became
larger than our
childhoods.

Expanding so big
that we have to roll
right out of this
place we used
to call home.

I Promise

to visit,
to call,
to text,
to write.

Maria hugs me
and says,

Always be you.

I choke back the
emotions
and reply,

You too.

My New Home

I cover my new desk
in photos,
in postcards from Marcy,
in notes from Maria.

My record of the past.

I look out
my new window
in my new dorm room
in my new city.

And I feel like I belong
here.

On My Own

Again.

I feel so much more
whole this
time around
in New York.

A person who knows
where the streets lead,
where you can stand
to feel the subway
give the pavement a
heartbeat.

Welcome

the sign reads.

Welcome to the NYU
Creative Writing Program.

I will always feel like I am on a beat.
Ready to get the latest scoop,
get down to the bottom line,
figure out the truth.

But if my time with Marcy
taught
me anything,
it's that
I've got stories
in me.

It's time to tell them.

WANT TO KEEP READING?

If you liked this book, check out another book
from West 44 Books:

EVERYTHING IT TAKES
BY SANDI VAN

ISBN: 9781978595545

MY CALLING

The loudspeaker calls us down:

> *All juniors and seniors*
> *report to the cafeteria*
> *for the college fair.*

We follow
like cattle.

Mooing in groups
large and small.

Chewing gum
and checking phones.

Not me.

I'm ready for this.

Questions neatly written
on the last page
of my English notebook.

I'm ready
to leave this town
in my dust.

CHECK OUT MORE BOOKS AT:

www.west44books.com

An imprint of Enslow Publishing

WEST **44** BOOKS™

About The Author

Dakota is a poet and writer who manages a queer café in New Hampshire. Dakota is an alumni of AmeriCorps National Civilian Community Corps, and served 10 months in the Southwest region of the country. They have previously published their own zine, *Term*, and have had their nonfiction published in *Crab Fat Magazine*. In their free time, they can be found volunteering as a facilitator for the local LGBTQ Youth Group, sipping on lattes, perusing around greenhouses, and browsing the local bookstores for their next great read! They live with their wife, Danielle, and their 32 houseplants in Dover, New Hampshire.